WEIRD PARENTS

AUDREY WOOD

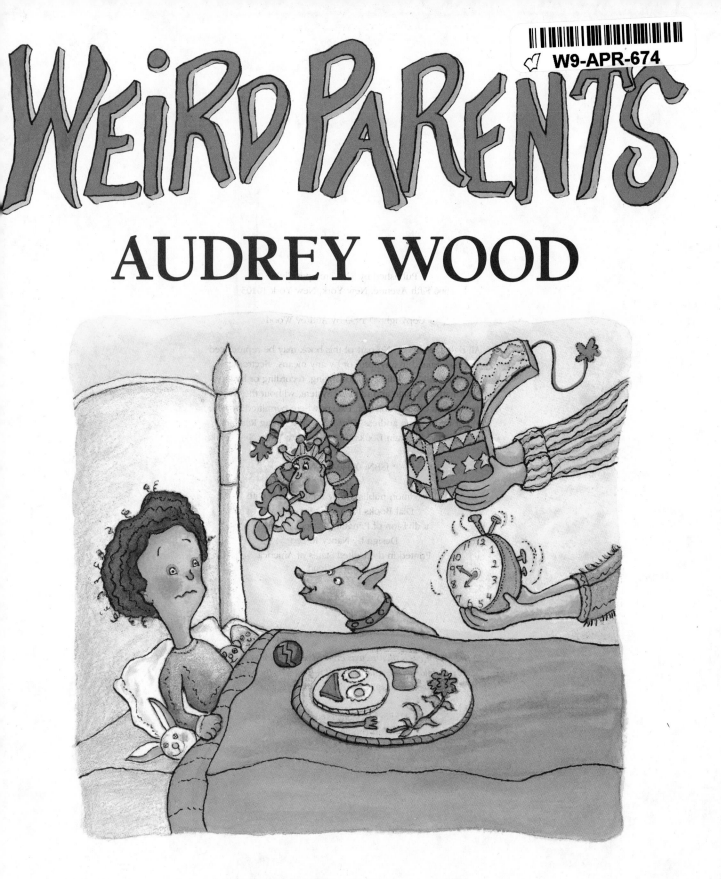

A TRUMPET CLUB SPECIAL EDITION

Published by The Trumpet Club
666 Fifth Avenue, New York, New York 10103

Copyright © 1990 by Audrey Wood

ISBN: 0-440-84449-5

This edition published by arrangement with
Dial Books for Young Readers,
a division of Penguin Books USA Inc.
Design by Nancy R. Leo
Printed in the United States of America
November 1990

10 9 8 7 6 5 4 3 2
UPC

*The art for each picture was created using colored pencils,
watercolor wash, and pen and ink. It was then color-
separated and reproduced in full color.*

PARCHEESI is a registered trademark of
Milton Bradley Company.

For Arthur Levine,
who has weird parents too.

There once was a boy who had
weird parents.
No matter how many times he told them not to,
the weird parents did weird things whenever
they went out into the world.

In the morning the weird mother always walked the boy to his bus stop.

"Bye-bye, honeycakes!" she'd call.

Then as the bus drove away, she'd blow a huge kiss and press her hand to her heart.

At twelve o'clock when the boy opened his lunchbox, he'd always have a weird surprise.

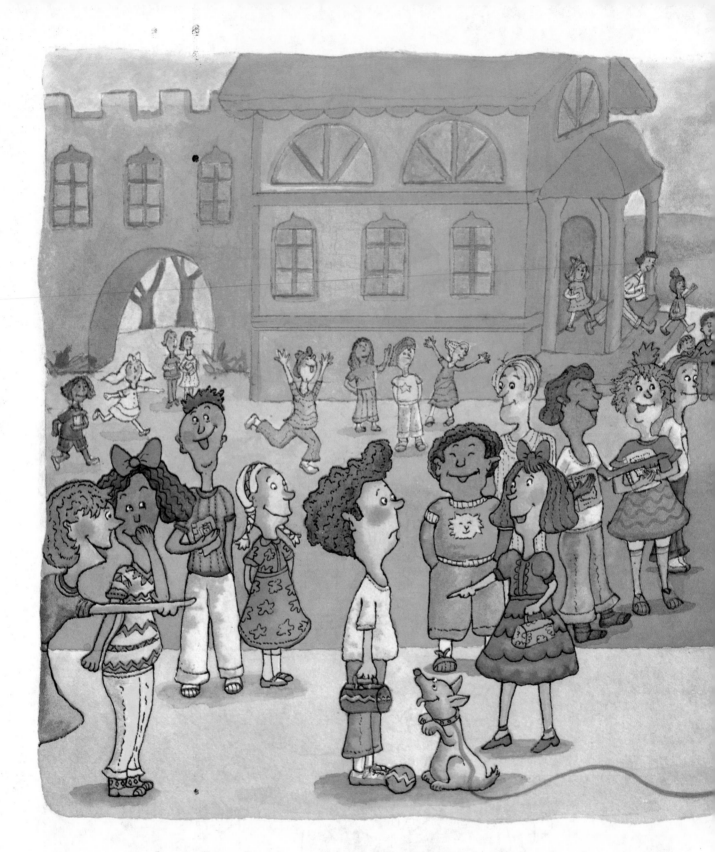

And in the afternoon the weird father always walked him home. But not before he shook hands with everyone he met.

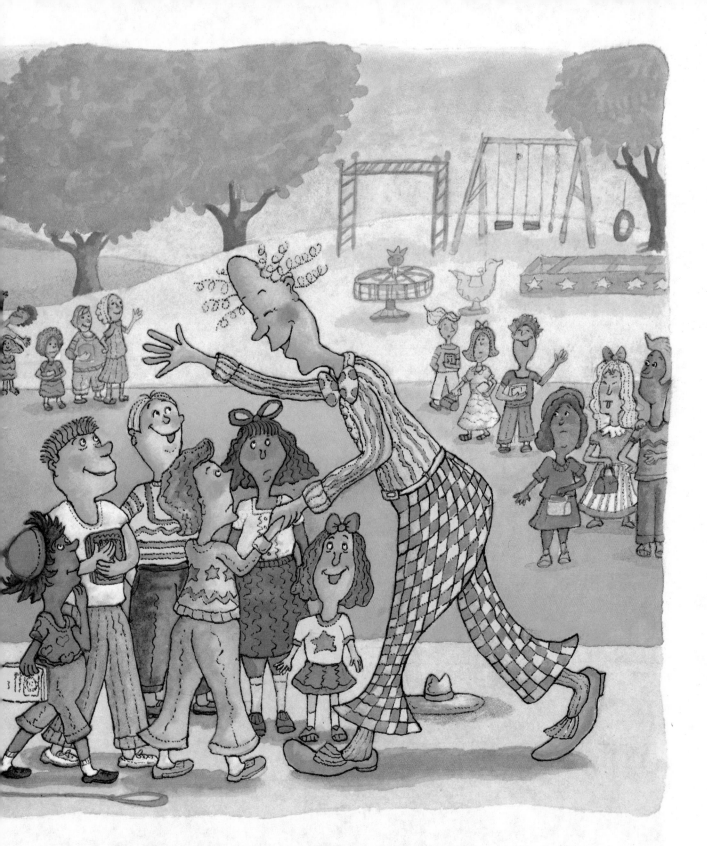

"Pleased to meet you. How do you do? Isn't it a
lovely day?" he'd say.

More than anything, the boy dreaded the family's
night out on the town. Every Saturday evening

the weird father put on his weird hat and the weird
mother combed her hair in a weird way.

Then they would dance all the way down the stairs
to their weird car.

They were always early for the picture show, so the
boy had to stand in line with them.

The weird mother always talked about the boy as if he wasn't there.

"My son has a belly button that sticks out. No one else in our family has one like it."

And the weird father always asked the boy to do
something silly.

"Walk like a chicken," he'd say.

Of course the boy wouldn't, so the weird father did
it instead.

When the movie began, the boy tried to enjoy it,

but his weird parents always laughed out loud when
no one else did.

At least things got better after the movie. The weird
father always treated them to ice cream cones. And the
weird mother always let the boy pick out a comic book.

At home they all played a double round of Parcheesi.®
And the weird parents never got mad if the boy won
both games.

And when they tucked him into bed and
kissed him good night, the weird parents always
sang a little song.

"Sweet dreams,
We love you,
Good night,
Now don't let the bedbugs bite,
Don't let the bedbugs bite."

But as the boy lay in bed trying to go to sleep, he couldn't help wishing his parents weren't weird anymore.

Then he wished everyone else had weird parents.

Yet he knew that wasn't possible.

And somehow it didn't matter....

After all...

they were his parents, weird or not.

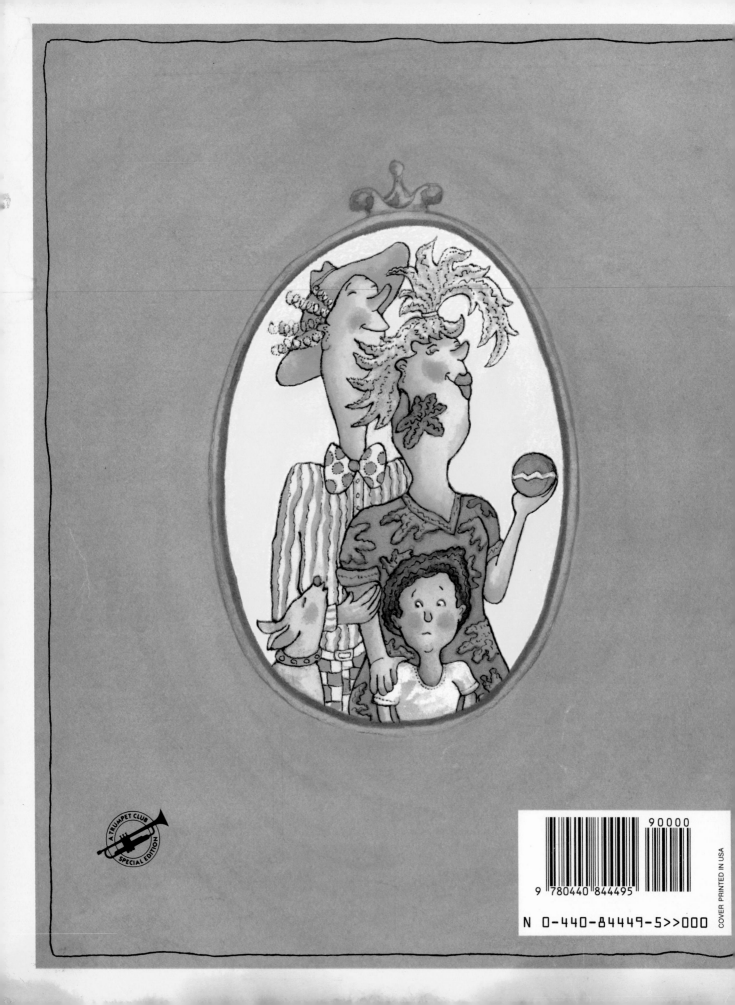

9 780440 844495

90000

N 0-440-84449-5>>000

COVER PRINTED IN USA